D1095644

BY LEA TADDONIO ILLUSTRATED BY ALESSIA TRUNFIO

LUCKY 8

#3 Deadwood Hill Strikes Back

Spellbound

An Imprint of Magic Wagon
abdopublishing.com

To Jarah, Bronte and Poppy — LT

To my Family, my Love, my best friends and Eva. Thank you all
for helping me to make it real in all your personal ways. — AT

abdopublishing.com

Published by Magic Wagon, a division of ABDO, PO Box 398166,
Minneapolis, Minnesota 55439. Copyright © 2018 by Abdo Consulting
Group, Inc. International copyrights reserved in all countries. No
part of this book may be reproduced in any form without written
permission from the publisher. Spellbound™ is a trademark and logo
of Magic Wagon.

Printed in the United States of America, North Mankato, Minnesota.
092017
012018

THIS BOOK CONTAINS
RECYCLED MATERIALS

Written by Lea Taddonio
Illustrated by Alessia Trunfio
Edited by Heidi M.D. Elston
Art Directed by Laura Mitchell

Publisher's Cataloging-in-Publication Data

Names: Taddonio, Lea, author. | Trunfio, Alessia, illustrator.
Title: Deadwood Hill strikes back / by Lea Taddonio; illustrated by Alessia Trunfio.
Description: Minneapolis, Minnesota : Magic Wagon, 2018. | Series: Lucky 8; Book 3
Summary: Makayla and Liam are able to talk to Jo Ann George through the Magic 8 Ball. She's
    trapped in another dimension called the Topsy-Turvy. The twins want to save her. Through
    the Magic 8 Ball, Jo Ann tells them how to get there. Will Makayla and Liam reach her in time?
Identifiers: LCCN 2017946550 | ISBN 9781532130557 (lib.bdg.) | ISBN 9781532131158 (ebook) |
    ISBN 9781532131455 (Read-to-me ebook)
Subjects: LCSH: Fantasy--Juvenile fiction. | Ghosts--Juvenile fiction. | Rescue work--Juvenile fiction. |
    Brothers and sisters--Juvenile fiction.
Classification: DDC [FIC]--dc23
LC record available at https://lccn.loc.gov/2017946550

TABLE OF CONTENTS

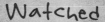

CHAPTER 1

Watched

Liam and I run home from school and push open the **creaky** front gate.

My brother stares up at Deadwood Hill. "Do you have the feeling someone is watching us?"

I nod as a SHIVER slides down my spine. The house's windows are dark, like holes in a SKULL. Black. Empty.

6

A young girl used to live here. Jo Ann George. A girl who was probably not much different from me and my twin. She DISAPPEARED, and her family moved from town.

But we've FOUND her.

Well, sort of.

"Let me see it," I tell Liam.

He doesn't even ask what "it" is.

He opens his backpack and passes me the Magic 8 Ball.

Maybe it's my imagination, but the plastic toy feels WARM. It's almost as if I'm touching a person's hand.

"Jo Ann?" I whisper, *shaking* the ball. "Jo Ann, **TALK** to us! Are you there?"

The white triangle *spins* in the window, faster and faster. Finally, it **STOPS**, spelling out a single word. *Yes.*

Before I can ask anything else,

the triangle begins to *spin* again.

"What is happening now?"

"I don't know." Liam's voice is

HIGHER than normal.

We SINK to the front step of
the porch, both **DIZZY**.

Help. She is going to find me.

"Who?" I **SHOUT**. "Jo Ann!

Who is HUNTING you?"

"Who, or *what?*" Liam takes off his glasses and rubs the lenses on his shirt. His **EYES** are big and round.

The triangle floats, not moving. No answer.

The world goes quiet except for a **RUMBLE** of thunder.

CHAPTER 2

Cold

Liam points to the **DARK** clouds covering the sun. "Let's get inside."

"No. Don't move. Jo Ann will come back." I shake the Magic 8 Ball. "Come on, tell us how to **HELP** you."

We **WAIT**.

Nothing.

The hair on the back of my neck

prickles. If this were one of my

favorite horror movies, SPOOKY

music would start playing.

The air smells like rain. A drop

hits me on the head. More thunder

BOOMS.

Liam jumps to his feet. "Come on.
This **STORM** is moving fast."

I know he is right. Yet my feet
don't want to take a step.

Something happened to Jo Ann.

Something bad.

She is **TRAPPED**.

She is being hunted.

I scream when a **BOLT** of lightning
STRIKES the field across the street.

"Makayla, move!" Liam pushes open

the door.

I run inside. I *pretend* the
lion-faced door knocker didn't just
seem to BLINK.

"Want a snack?" Liam walks to the kitchen.

"How can you even THINK about food at a time like this?" My own stomach feels sick.

Liam shrugs. "When I'm SCARED, chocolate helps." He OPENS the fridge and takes out a carton of chocolate milk.

I pick up the Magic 8 Ball again.

"Jo Ann! Jo Ann, where are you?"

Rain **SPLATTERS** the windows.

The air feels COLD. So very COLD. But

the Magic 8 Ball is warming up.

I turn to Liam. He **DUNKS** a cookie

in his glass.

"She's back!" I *SHOUT*.

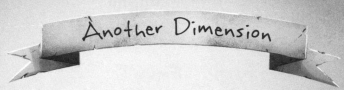

CHAPTER 3

Another Dimension

She is coming. The **CREEPY** sentence appears in the Magic 8 Ball's WINDOW.

Please come find me!

"Jo Ann, calm down. *Focus*. Where are you?" I am pacing the kitchen.

Her answer doesn't make sense.

I'm in the Topsy-Turvy.

Liam scratches his head. He *GLANCES* around the room. "What's the Topsy-Turvy?"

The Magic 8 Ball's window GLOWS with a pale blue light. *Here. Not here. Close. Far. Inside. Outside. Everywhere. Nowhere.*

My brother and I exchange
frowns. That's when a **LIGHT BULB**
goes off in the back of my mind.
"Wait. Jo Ann, is the Topsy-Turvy
another **DIMENSION?**"

"*Huh?*" Liam stuffs another cookie in his mouth. "What is a DIMENSION?"

"A DIMENSION is a parallel universe.

A whole nother space that is right next

to our world." I wave my hand in the

empty air. "But INVISIBLE."

The house shakes from the wind.

More thunder.

"Wow. This STORM doesn't

feel right," Liam says.

I bite my lip. **FOG** is heavy in the yard. The rain comes down sideways. "Liam, we have to figure out a way to get into the Topsy-Turvy."

A blue light **GLEAMS** from the Magic 8 Ball again. *You must eat an apple from the tree.*

The witch's tree rises through the big window. The dead branch looks *ghostly* white against the black clouds. Two red apples dangle from the end.

I **GULP**. Those two delicious-looking apples weren't there this morning.

"Come on," I tell my brother and head for the front door.

"But, once we get into the Topsy-Turvy . . ." **WORRY** lines appear between my brother's eyebrows. "Can we get back **OUT**?"

CHAPTER 4

Hurry!

The Magic 8 Ball isn't just warm. Now it's **HOT**. The plastic is hard to hold on to without dropping.

Hurry! The triangle reads. *It's almost too late.*

I don't take another breath until I'm in the front yard. Rain *STINGS* my cheeks. The witch's tree waves in the wind.

I **HEAVE** a sigh of relief when Liam appears beside me.

He notices and grins. "Hey, Sis. Can't let you go without me."

"Thank you," I say and mean it. The Magic 8 Ball seems to PULSE.

We grab the tree and begin to CLIMB.

UP and UP and UP we go. I can see
my bed and posters from up here.

Those make-believe monsters look
a little silly now. Where we are
going there could be actual monsters.

Anything is possible in a place
called the Topsy-Turvy.

Carefully, we **SCOOT** along
the branch and each pick an apple.

"Ready?" I ask Liam. The fruit is
red as **blood**.

"One," he says.

"Two," I answer.

"Three!" We shout and each take a big bite. There is a bright flash. A 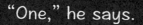.

Lightning strikes the tree.

And then . . . we VANISH.